ORCA
Echoes

JUSTINE McKEEN
WALK the TALK

Sigmund Brouwer
illustrated by Dave Whamond

ORCA BOOK

Savannah—this one is especially for you.

Text copyright © 2012 Sigmund Brouwer
Illustrations copyright © 2012 Dave Whamond

Library and Archives Canada Cataloguing in Publication

Brouwer, Sigmund, 1959-
Justine McKeen, walk the talk / Sigmund Brouwer ;
illustrated by Dave Whamond.
(Orca echoes)

Issued also in electronic format.
ISBN 978-1-55469-929-2

I. Whamond, Dave II. Title. III. Series: Orca echoes
PS8553.R68467J884 2012   JC813'.54   C2011-907543-1

First published in the United States, 2012
Library of Congress Control Number: 2011942591

Summary: Justine has plans to start a walking school bus at her school to help create
a greener environment, but not everyone trusts her ideas.

Orca Book Publishers gratefully acknowledges the support for its publishing programs
provided by the following agencies: the Government of Canada through the Canada Book
Fund and the Canada Council for the Arts, and the Province of British Columbia
through the BC Arts Council and the Book Publishing Tax Credit.

MIX
Paper from
responsible sources
FSC® C004071

ANCIENT FOREST ™
FRIENDLY

*Orca Book Publishers is dedicated to preserving the environment and has printed this book
on paper certified by the Forest Stewardship Council®.*

Cover artwork and interior illustrations by Dave Whamond
Author photo by Reba Baskett

ORCA BOOK PUBLISHERS
PO Box 5626, Stn. B
Victoria, BC Canada
V8R 6S4

ORCA BOOK PUBLISHERS
PO Box 468
Custer, WA USA
98240-0468

www.orcabook.com
Printed and bound in Canada.

15 14 13 12 • 4 3 2 1

Chapter One

"I wish all cars had smoke coming out of them like that," Justine McKeen said to her friends Michael and Safdar. She pointed at an old car passing them on their way to school. A long trail of blue-black smoke followed behind it.

"What?" Safdar said. "You're the Queen of Green! An old car like that should be taken off the road!"

The three of them had almost reached the school. There were only a few minutes until the bell rang to start the day.

"Yes," Justine said. "I am the Queen of Green. And yes, that car should be taken off the road. But look at all the cars in front of our school."

A long line of cars idled as kids were being dropped off. There was also a lineup of buses. Kids exited the buses and ran into the school. "Do you see all the stuff coming out of those cars?"

"Those cars are a lot newer than that old one," Michael said.

"Just because we don't see any black smoke doesn't make them better. All of these cars are sending invisible stuff called carbon dioxide into the air. Too much carbon dioxide is bad for the environment. Did you know, if nine kids walk to school all year instead of going in cars or buses, it stops over a ton of carbon dioxide from going into the air? It also saves gas. The less gas we use, the less we have to drill for oil. And that's good too. Plus walking is healthier for kids."

"Let me guess," Safdar said. "You have a plan. Again."

"Of course I do," Justine said. "I am the Queen of Green."

"Let's hope it's a better plan than your last one," Safdar said. "I still can't believe you talked us into helping you move all that dirt to start a roof garden at school."

"Speaking of the garden," Michael said, "don't look now, but the janitor is up on the roof. And he doesn't seem happy to see you, Justine."

When someone says, "Don't look," the first thing a person does is look. So Safdar and Justine looked up at the roof. Mr. Noble, the janitor, had climbed a ladder to get to the top. His hands were on his hips. He frowned at all three of them.

"Hi, Mr. Noble!" Justine waved. "Nice to see you!"

"It's not nice to see you," he yelled.

"I already said I'm sorry! Can I help clean up the mess?" Justine asked.

"You stay away from me! Your help would only make it worse!"

Michael and Safdar tried pulling Justine inside the school.

"Everybody is staring at us," Safdar said.

"It's your hat," Michael said to Justine.

Justine wore a wide-brimmed hat with a stuffed bird perched on the side.

She smiled. "I like my hat. It goes with my dress."

"I'm afraid to ask," Safdar said, "but what's your plan for those cars? Plug all the exhaust pipes with bananas?"

"Good idea," Justine said. "Or maybe a potato. We just sneak up behind each car and—"

"I was joking," Safdar said. "Please don't try that. Something could go very wrong. Just like the garden on the school roof went wrong."

"How would I know two days of rain would make the dirt so heavy?" Justine said. "And how many times does a person have to say sorry?"

Chapter Two

"Don't look now," Michael said to Justine and Safdar. "There's the school bully, Jimmy Blatzo."

Whenever someone says, "Don't look," the first thing a person does is look. So Safdar and Justine looked. Jimmy Blatzo was beside the water fountain by their classroom.

"Hey, Blatzo," Justine said.

"Quit calling me Blatzo," Jimmy Blatzo said.

"I know, I know." Justine grinned. "If I call you Blatzo, people might think I'm not scared of you."

"You just said it again." Jimmy Blatzo shook his head. "I have to get going. You've got the same substitute teacher my class had last week.

He is a jerk. I don't want him to know I'm in the hallway."

"How come?" Michael asked.

"Look, kid, did I give you permission to talk to me?" Blatzo asked.

"Um, no," said Michael.

"Then don't talk to me," said Jimmy Blatzo.

"Got it," Michael said.

"That's still talking," Jimmy Blatzo said.

Michael silently mouthed the word *Sorry*.

"Much better," Jimmy Blatzo said.

"Hey, Blatzo," Justine said. "What's the deal with the substitute teacher? Why don't you want him to know you're in the hallway?"

"You'll find out," Jimmy Blatzo told her. "And quit calling me Blatzo."

"Sure." Justine walked toward her classroom. Then she turned back. "Hey, Blatzo. What do you think of my hat?"

"A bird," he said. "You always dress weird."

"Thanks for the compliment," she said. "I like it too."

Chapter Three

The substitute teacher's name was Mr. Barnes. He was tall and skinny and had long stringy hair. He wore a black T-shirt with the name of a rock band on it.

The bell rang, and all the students sat down. Mr. Barnes sat behind his desk. He pointed at Justine. "Put your hat in a cage before it flies away," he said.

Justine put her hat under her desk.

"That was funny," he said to the class. "Why aren't you laughing?"

"She is our friend," Safdar said. "It's not nice to make fun of the way she dresses."

Mr. Barnes stood. He glared at Safdar. "What is your name?"

"Michael," Safdar said. "If you have to put a red mark beside my name, I will understand."

Now the class laughed.

That made Mr. Barnes angrier. "What's so funny?"

Michael put up his hand. "I am Michael."

"Hah, hah," Mr. Barnes said. "Sure. Very funny."

Mr. Barnes sat down and opened a newspaper. "It is silent reading time. Yesterday you read chapter one. Today read chapter two. And keep quiet."

Then Mr. Barnes made a loud noise. It was the kind of noise that happens when a person's body lets out some gas. It was an F-A-R-T-I-N-G noise.

The class started laughing again.

"Enough!" Mr. Barnes said.

As soon as the class was quiet, Mr. Barnes made the same noise, an F-A-R-T-I-N-G noise, except in a higher pitch. It sounded like someone had stepped on a duck.

The class laughed louder.

"Enough!" Mr. Barnes roared. He reached under his chair and pulled out a small machine with a tiny speaker. It had been taped under his seat. He looked at it, and it made another loud, rude noise, an F-A-R-T-I-N-G noise.

On the side of the machine, white letters spelled two words: *Farting Machine*.

"Whoever did this is going straight to the principal," he yelled at the class. "Otherwise, everyone in the class has extra homework."

Justine McKeen stood up. She put on her hat. "You can send me to the principal," she said.

"What's your name?" Mr. Barnes asked.

"Justine McKeen," she said.

"The Queen of Green!" said Safdar.

"Well, now she's the Queen of In Trouble With the Principal. Go to the office right now. I will be there in a minute to explain what happened."

Chapter Four

Justine sat on a chair outside the open door to the principal's office. She heard the janitor, Mr. Noble, talking to the principal.

"Ms. Booth, I have a problem. In this school there are girls who put on lipstick and then kiss the mirrors in the girls' bathrooms," Mr. Noble said. "They leave big smooch marks on the mirrors."

"Smooch marks?" Ms. Booth said.

"Smooch marks. In all shades of colors," said Mr. Noble.

"Well," she said, "it's probably better to kiss mirrors than to kiss boys."

"You may think it's funny. But I don't. After school every day it takes over half an hour to wipe the lipstick off the mirrors. That stuff is not easy to remove. Can't you do something?"

"I will give it some thought," Ms. Booth said. "How is it going with the hole in the roof?"

"You mean where the roof garden was?"

"We've been through this, George. It was my fault. I did tell Justine I thought it was a good idea. A roof gets lots of sunshine, and it's not a place rabbits or deer can get at. I just didn't expect she would go ahead with it."

"Face it," Mr. Noble said. "That girl is weird. You should see the hat she wore today."

"I'm out here!" Justine said from her chair. "And the hat matches my dress perfectly. It's to remind people about birds and to not harm them."

"I like the way you dress," Ms. Booth called out to Justine. "It reminds me of a flower child from the peace movement."

14

"Thanks. That's what my grammy says," Justine said.

Mr. Barnes stormed into the room. He was holding the Farting Machine. He marched past Justine in to Ms. Booth's office.

"Thanks for knocking," Ms. Booth said.

"That girl out there taped this under my chair," Mr. Barnes said. "Justine Queen Green, or whatever her name is."

"I'm not surprised," Mr. Noble said. "I'm telling you. The girl is weird."

"George, that's enough," Ms. Booth said. "And Mr. Barnes, what are you holding?"

"It makes sounds," he said.

"What kind of sounds?" asked Ms. Booth.

"Going-to-the-bathroom sounds," said Mr. Barnes. "Like this—"

Justine heard an F-A-R-T-I-N-G noise. She hoped Mr. Barnes had made the noise with his mouth.

"I see," Ms. Booth said. "And you say that Justine McKeen put it under your chair."

"She confessed. I demand you punish her!"

"And it would be nice if you did something about the smooch marks," Mr. Noble said. "Maybe that was Justine's idea too. Smooching mirrors to save the planet."

"Smooch marks?" Mr. Barnes said. "What kind of school is this?"

Justine heard Ms. Booth sigh. "Goodbye, gentlemen."

Both of them stomped out of the principal's office and stopped to glare at Justine.

"You are a weird, weird girl," Mr. Noble said to Justine. "With weird, weird ideas."

Then they stomped out into the hall. It was Justine's turn to talk to Ms. Booth.

Chapter Five

"I see these more often than you might guess," Ms. Booth said. She was holding the speaker that Mr. Barnes had found under his desk. "It's a remote-control farting machine. I take them away from Jimmy Blatzo all the time. He gets a new one whenever he can save enough money. I happen to think they are funny. But only when it's appropriate. Do you think it's appropriate to tape one under a teacher's chair?"

"No," said Justine.

"Why did you do it?" Ms. Booth asked.

Justine didn't answer.

"Well," Ms. Booth said, "at least tell me where the remote control is. I'll need to take that from you too."

"Um," said Justine.

"You don't have the remote control, do you?"

"Um," Justine said again.

"That's what I thought," Ms. Booth said. "You don't even know it needs a remote. This doesn't seem like the type of thing you would do. So the question is, why did you confess to doing it if you didn't?"

"Mr. Barnes said everyone would get punished if no one stood up. So I thought I would save everyone else from trouble. Plus, Mr. Barnes said he would send whoever did it to the principal. I thought it would be a good way to get to talk to you. I've been trying to meet with you, but the secretary keeps telling me you are too busy."

"Oh."

"Are you too busy to talk to me because you are mad about my idea for a garden on the roof?"

"I admit it seems like every day you try to bring me an idea to help the school go green. Remember, I asked you to write them down instead of coming to see me all the time?"

"Did you read the letters I sent you?"

Ms. Booth grabbed the first three letters off the pile. "Not all of them."

"That's why I wanted to see you. I have a really, really good idea this time. Could you listen to just one more? Please?"

Ms. Booth smiled and nodded. "If it was important enough to take the blame for something you didn't do, I suppose I should hear what you have to say. What is your next idea?"

"A walking school bus," Justine said.

A funny look crossed Ms. Booth's face.

"I don't mean school buses with legs. I mean instead of kids taking a bus to school, they walk. Together. In a group. Too many people talk about helping the environment but never do it. I think it's time to walk the talk."

Ms. Booth leaned forward. "You have two minutes. Tell me your idea."

Chapter Six

"It is really good for the planet," Justine said. "And it's good for kids too. A walking school bus doesn't use gasoline, and it doesn't send engine exhaust into the air. Kids will get extra exercise every day. Plus they will have fun talking with their friends as they walk through the neighborhood. A grown-up leads the walking school bus. The grown-up is called a driver, but really the driver just walks with everyone else."

"Setting it up sounds like a lot of work," Ms. Booth said.

"No," Justine said. "All you have to do is create a walking-school-bus route. Each route would have nine kids on it. You make sure the route has as few streets as possible to cross. The driver would stop at the first kid's house, and then move on to the next kid's house. The walking school bus would arrive at the same time every day, just like a real school bus with a real schedule. The only difference is the kids walk instead of riding the bus. It would be great if our school could organize at least ten walking school buses."

"Sorry," Ms. Booth said. "If it is a school activity, I would need signed permission slips from the parents."

"I already found walking-school-bus permission slips on the Internet. I printed them out for you."

"Sorry," Ms. Booth said. "If it is a school activity, the students will need adult supervision."

"A walking school bus works like a train," Justine said. "You have one parent at the front of the bus and one parent at the back of the bus."

"Sorry," Ms. Booth said. "That would require two parents every day. We can't afford to pay them."

"If they are volunteers," Justine said, "you don't have to pay them. And the school will save money if you don't need to run a real school bus."

"Sorry," Ms. Booth said. "I don't have time to do all the work to get it started."

"That's okay," Justine said. "I will do all the work. I will plan the route. I will find kids who will join the walking school bus. I'll make sure to get all the permission slips signed. I will even go door to door and get a list of adults who will volunteer to supervise every day."

"Sorry," Ms. Booth said. "What if the weather is bad?"

"I have already found someone to donate umbrellas," Justine said.

"It sounds like you have everything covered," Ms. Booth said. "Let me think about it."

"Thank you," Justine said.

"Okay." Ms. Booth grinned. "I've thought about it. Let's do it!"

Chapter Seven

Justine's first stop for a parent volunteer was at the home of Sydney Martin, a girl in her class.

Sydney's house was down the street from Justine's. It had a fenced yard and a gate. Justine opened the gate and saw Sydney's little brother Adam sitting on the grass with a cat in his arms.

"Hey, Adam," Justine said.

"Hey, Justine," Adam said. "Can you hold Snuggles for me?"

Justine sat beside Adam. "Sure. I like cats."

"Thank you." Adam gave the cat to Justine.

Snuggles began to purr in Justine's arms. Adam lifted the cat's tail.

"What are you doing?" Justine asked.

"Snuggles is chapped," Adam said. "Just like how my mom's lips are dry."

Adam held the cat's tail high. He took a tube of lip balm and rubbed it on the cat's behind.

"Oh!" Justine said. "I don't know if that's a good idea."

"I do it all the time," Adam said. "Snuggles likes it."

The door to the house opened. "There you are, Adam. I've been looking everywhere for you," said Mrs. Martin. She walked down the steps.

Justine handed the cat to Adam and stood.

"Hello, Mrs. Martin," Justine said. "Did you get the information about a walking school bus? I wanted to save paper, so I emailed it to you. I am looking for parent helpers. It will be good for the planet."

"I can't remember," Mrs. Martin said. "I am very busy." Mrs. Martin looked at Adam. "That's where my lip balm went. Give it back, please."

Adam stood and handed Mrs. Martin the lip balm.

"What is a walking school bus?" Mrs. Martin asked Justine. She took the lid off the lip balm. Then she raised it to her lips.

"Don't do that!" Justine said.

Too late. Mrs. Martin smeared the lip balm across her lips.

"The lip balm," Justine said. "Adam just used it on Snuggles."

"Ew," Mrs. Martin said. "He put it on Snuggles's mouth?"

"No," Justine said. "The other end."

"What!" Mrs. Martin said.

"Under Snuggles's tail," Adam said proudly. "Where it is all dry. Snuggles likes it."

Mrs. Martin wiped her lips with the back of her hand. She spat and spat and spat. When she was finished, her face was very red.

Mrs. Martin glared at Justine. "I saw you holding Snuggles. You helped Adam do that!"

"No," Justine said. "I didn't—"

"I know all about you, Miss Queen of Green. I suppose you think helping little boys put lip balm on a cat's behind is good for the planet too?"

"No. I—"

"You are a weird girl," said Mrs. Martin. "Please go away and don't come back."

Chapter Eight

Justine's next stop was at the home of Ava Free, another girl in her class. Everybody knew that her dad, Mr. Free, liked everything neat and perfect. He had the best lawn in town and said it was only for looking at, not for walking across.

Before walking up to the door, Justine stopped at the curb. A recycling box was waiting for pickup alongside some garbage cans. She looked inside the recycling box.

"This is good," Justine said to herself. "Papers. And bottles."

She lifted the garbage can's lid and began to pull out garbage. "Very good. Very very good. This is giving me an idea."

Mr. Free drove up and parked his shiny car in front of the house. When he got out, he saw a tiny spot on the hood. He rubbed it with his sleeve until the hood was shiny and perfect, like the rest of his car.

He marched up to Justine. "What are you doing in our garbage?" he said.

Justine held out her hand for a handshake. "Hello, Mr. Free," she said. "It is nice to see you. My name is Justine McKeen. I am in your daughter's class at school."

"I'm not shaking your hand," he said. "It is dirty. And it is dirty because it's been in my garbage. And the garbage is on my perfect lawn!"

"You have nice garbage," Justine said. "It is giving me an idea."

"How about this for an idea. You put all that garbage back in the can. It is on my perfect lawn!"

"Of course," Justine said. "You should be proud of yourself. None of your garbage can be recycled.

And everything in your recycle box can be recycled. Many people don't sort their garbage or recycling, which gives me an idea."

"I don't care what your idea is," Mr. Free said. "You shouldn't dig through other people's garbage. Or put it on their perfect lawn!"

"Could I paint your recycling box gold?" Justine asked.

"What?"

"My idea is to give people who do a good job recycling gold recycling boxes. Like when kids get gold stars at school."

"My idea is that you stay out of my garbage," Mr. Free said. "You are a weird, weird girl. Please go away."

Chapter Nine

The next day after school, Justine, Safdar and Michael sat at a table outside Ice-Cream Heaven. It was owned by Mr. Tait. Mr. Tait was Justine's friend. He had helped her with a greenhouse project.

"This is not good," Safdar said.

"Are you kidding?" Michael told him. "Your ice-cream cone is two scoops of chocolate, covered with chocolate sprinkles. How could it not be good?"

"I meant this is not good that Justine is so quiet. Look, she's not even eating her ice cream."

Justine had not said a word since leaving school. She had only nodded when Mr. Tait asked if she wanted strawberry ice cream on her cone.

"I know you meant it is not good that Justine is so quiet," Michael said to Safdar. "I was trying to make a joke."

"Because she's so quiet?" Safdar asked.

"Yes, because she's so quiet. I've never seen her like this."

"I'm ready to talk," Justine said.

"Good!" Safdar said.

"Good!" Michael said.

"But after I do," Justine said, "I might not talk for the rest of my life."

"What?" Safdar said.

"What?" Michael said.

"That way I won't make people mad anymore." She looked at both of them. "Don't lie to me. People think I'm weird, right? I can't get any

36

parents to volunteer for the walking school bus. If I don't get any parent volunteers, no walking school bus."

"Yes, people think you are a little weird," Michael said.

"Just a little?" Justine asked.

"Maybe a tiny bit more than just a little," Safdar said. "You don't dress normal. And you are always coming up with ideas for being green."

Justine looked at Michael. "Do you two think I'm weird?"

"A little," Michael said.

"Just a little?"

"Maybe a tiny bit more than just a little," Safdar said.

"Oh," Justine said. Her strawberry ice cream was melting. "Since you are being so truthful, is there anything else?"

"Well…" Michael said.

"Well, what?" said Justine.

"Well," Safdar said, "everybody knows you talk a little too much and you boss us around a little too much and that you sometimes don't tell all of the truth. And—"

Justine got up and threw her ice cream into the garbage and ran away.

"And that's why we like you so much!" Safdar yelled.

But Justine didn't hear. She was running too fast.

Chapter Ten

Justine didn't stop running until she reached the park.

She sat on a bench near some bushes. She didn't want anyone to see the tears on her face.

A black dog in the park trotted up to the bench. While she was crying, she scratched the dog's head. It jumped onto the bench and licked her face.

"Thanks," Justine said. "At least you don't care that I'm weird."

The dog licked her face again. She scratched the dog between its ears. The dog thumped its tail.

"Maybe I'll just come here every day after school and meet you," Justine said. "I'll never talk to anyone else. That way I won't say anything weird or do anything weird that gets me in trouble. Would that be okay with you?"

The dog licked her face again.

"Seems like a yes to me," Justine said. She stopped crying and put her arm around the dog. "After all," Justine said, "you don't think I'm weird. And this is a nice park. Maybe you can help me pick up the litter. It will be just you and me trying to help the planet."

An old woman walked toward them. The woman used a cane. She wore glasses.

"Hello," Justine said to the woman as she walked in front of them.

"Hello," the woman said. "What is your name?"

"Justine McKeen."

"Are you the girl I heard about who digs through people's garbage?"

"Well—"

"And who helped a little boy put lip balm on a cat's behind?"

"Well—"

A loud rude noise erupted underneath Justine. It sounded as if someone had stepped on a duck. It was an F-A-R-T-I-N-G noise.

"How rude!" the woman said.

"It's not me," Justine said. "Really."

The noise started again. It was louder. This time it sounded as if air was coming out of a balloon.

"Rude!" the woman said. "And don't blame it on the dog."

Before Justine could say a word, another F-A-R-T-I-N-G noise as loud as a trumpet erupted from under the bench.

"You are a weird, weird girl," the woman said. She stomped away as fast as she could with her cane.

Jimmy Blatzo stepped out of the bushes behind the bench. He was laughing. He was also holding a remote control.

"That was the funniest thing I ever saw," he said. "This bench is a perfect place for that trick."

"Go away, Blazto," Justine said. "Now that woman thinks I'm weird. Just like everyone else."

"Not everyone," Jimmy Blatzo said. "Okay, nearly everyone."

"Do you think I'm weird?"

"You do make cricket brownies. And you did put a garden on the school roof."

"Go away, Blazto." Justine started crying again. "I don't want you to see me cry."

"I already saw you cry. That's why I used my remote control. I was trying to make you laugh."

"You just made me look even weirder than I am. Tomorrow, I'm going to wear normal clothes to school. I will never do anything to make me look different again."

"Your friends like you the way you are," Jimmy said. "Really."

"Go away, Blazto. I don't need people like you. All I need is this dog."

Jimmy Blazto grabbed his farting machine from under the bench and walked away.

Justine McKeen held the dog and sobbed for a long time.

Chapter Eleven

The next morning, Justine walked to school by herself. She wore a purple hat with a fake flower hanging over the brim. Her sweater was pink with blue polka dots. And her skirt was bright orange.

She was ready for everyone to tease her. But no one in front of the school noticed her.

That's because Jimmy Blatzo was walking up and down the sidewalk, carrying a big sign. The sign said, WE WANT A WALKING BUS!

Michael was behind him. He was carrying a sign too. It said, MORE WALKING, LESS DRIVING!

Safdar was behind Michael. Safdar's sign said, HELP US SET UP OUR FIRST WALKING SCHOOL BUS—THEN A BUNCH MORE!!

And behind Safdar, another fifty students walked with signs too. All of them waved their signs at the drivers in their cars.

Justine walked up to Jimmy Blatzo. "Hey, Blatzo," she said. "What is going on?"

"Quit calling me Blatzo," he said. "And take this sign. We've been waiting for you to lead us."

He pulled out a sign that was hidden behind his own. The sign said, LET'S WALK THE TALK ABOUT GOING GREEN.

Justine looked at Jimmy Blatzo. "I don't understand."

"You don't understand how important it is to be green? Michael, Safdar and I worked for hours last night to make these signs. Then we called everyone."

"I don't understand why you are doing this," said Justine.

"We are your friends," Jimmy Blatzo said. "We like you the way you are. You didn't give us a chance to tell you that. So we decided to show you. Right, Michael? Right, Safdar?"

"Right!" Safdar said.

"Right!" Michael said.

"Did I give you permission to talk?" Jimmy Blazto asked Michael and Safdar.

Michael and Safdar mouthed the word *Sorry*.

"Much better," Jimmy Blatzo said.

Justine laughed. Everything was back to normal.

"By the way," Jimmy Blatzo told her. "Nice hat."

"I like it," Justine said. Justine took the sign and began to walk up and down the sidewalk with her friends.

"Didn't you tell me you were going to dress like everyone else from now on?" Jimmy Blatzo asked.

"I did," Justine said. "But when I looked in the mirror this morning, I decided it is more important to try to help the planet than it is to worry about what people think about me. So I changed, and I wore this instead."

Chapter Twelve

It rained on the first day of the walking school bus.

But it didn't matter. Justine McKeen had ten giant umbrellas. Each umbrella had *Ice-Cream Heaven* written on it. Mr. Tait had donated all the umbrellas so he could advertise.

Mrs. Martin was at the front of the walking school bus. She felt bad for yelling at Justine. She had learned that Adam had been using lip balm on the cat for a long time. She didn't feel good about all the times she had used the lip balm, but she felt good about apologizing to Justine.

Mr. Free was at the back of the walking school bus. He had decided it would be a good idea to have a gold recycling bin after all. That way his neighbors who knew he cared about his lawn would also know he cared about the environment.

The walking school bus was a lot of fun. Justine was somewhere in the middle. She had eight other kids to talk with and splash through puddles with.

It was the first walking school bus at their school. A lot of drivers honked to say hello as they passed. Everyone thought it was great that kids cared about the environment enough to ask for a walking school bus.

Justine thought the walking school bus was a success.

It was even better when they arrived at the school. After all the walking school bus passengers shook off their umbrellas, the janitor walked up to them.

"Hello, Mr. Barnes," Justine said. "We will do our best not to make a mess with the wet umbrellas."

"That's okay, Justine," Mr. Barnes said. "I just came to say thank you. I think the idea you gave me yesterday to stop the girls from putting lipstick

on the bathroom mirrors is going to work. How did you think of it?"

"I saw what happened with a little boy, a cat named Snuggles and a tube of lip balm," Justine said. "Maybe someday I will tell you about it."

"Well, your idea to stop the lipstick on the mirrors is so good, I'll be very surprised if I ever have to clean off any more smooch marks."

"I hope you're right," Justine said. "I want to make up for the extra work you had to do when the roof garden wrecked the roof."

"Don't worry," Mr. Barnes said. "I've decided it's important to be green, and a person needs to keep trying out different ideas." He winked at Justine. "I hope your class enjoys the video."

Chapter Thirteen

Justine's teacher, Mrs. Howie, rolled out the class television. She put a DVD in the player.

"Students," Mrs. Howie said. "Our principal has asked that every class watch this DVD. There has been a problem with girls putting lipstick marks on the bathroom mirrors. This DVD has a message from our principal and the janitor."

Mrs. Howie turned off the lights and pressed *Play*.

On the screen, Ms. Booth was holding a video camera and pointing it at a mirror in one of the girls' bathrooms. Her reflection appeared in the mirror.

She zoomed in on the smooch marks on the mirror. "This has become a problem because it is a lot of work for our janitor, Mr. Barnes. I thought I would show you how difficult it is for him to clean the mirror."

Ms. Booth turned the video camera toward Mr. Barnes. He wore rubber gloves. He was holding a large sponge. He waved at the camera. Then he spoke.

"I know it is fun for girls to kiss the mirrors," Mr. Barnes said. "But these marks are not fun to clean. The first thing I do is get this sponge wet. I like to recycle water instead of wasting it from the tap."

The video camera followed him as he walked to a toilet. He pushed the sponge into the toilet water. When he lifted the sponge out, toilet water dripped from the sponge.

"Next," Mr. Barnes said, "I use this sponge to clean the mirror."

With the sponge full of toilet water, he walked to the mirror. He washed the mirror with the sponge. Toilet water dripped down the mirror. When the

lipstick marks were finally gone, he squeezed the sponge out over the sink. Then he wiped the mirror again with the sponge to get the last of the toilet water off.

"Every day after school, I have to clean the mirrors with toilet water," Mr. Barnes said. "So now you know how much work it is for me. And you can help me by not kissing the mirrors anymore. Thank you."

The video ended.

Mrs. Howie turned the lights on and the television off.

"Girls," she said, "do you have any questions about the message from our janitor?"

Three girls put their hands up.

"Yes," Mrs. Howie said to the first girl.

Sydney Martin's eyes bulged. "Can I go to the bathroom? I have to brush my teeth! Right now!"

Ava had her hand over her mouth and said, "Me too! Please! Right now! I can't believe he uses toilet water to clean the mirror!"

Then the third girl, Mya, said, "Please! Right now! I feel sick."

Justine tried not to giggle. She knew they had kissed the mirror.

She also knew they would never do it again.

JUSTINE McKEEN
WALK the TALK

Notes for Students and Teachers

Chapter One

Many schools have No Idling signs outside them. Not only does this help the environment, but it prevents kids from breathing unhealthy air. If you think this is a problem at your school, you could ask your teacher about trying to put up No Idling signs. But ask nice!

Chapter Four

Roof gardens are a great idea, and they are becoming more and more popular. Often roofs that are black take more energy to cool, so putting plants on the roof saves energy. Plants convert carbon dioxide into oxygen, so the more plants there are, the better. If you think it's possible to start a roof garden at your school, just make sure you do it with your teachers and not the way Justine did.

Chapter Six

If you have a lot of students who live close enough to your school to be able to walk, it would be a great project to start a walking school bus. As you saw with Justine, it takes planning, parent volunteers and permission slips. You can also start a bicycle train, and it's just as much fun. Here's a website with all you need to get started: www.walkingschoolbus.org.

Chapter Ten

It's a little thing, but did you notice that Justine decided she was going to pick up litter while the dog kept her company in the park. Keep your eyes open for any pieces of litter you see. If every student in your school picked up one piece of litter a day, that would make a huge difference.

Chapter Twelve

Have a fun discussion with your teacher about when it might be appropriate for students to try to influence grown-ups by marching in a public place with signs.

 ## Chapter Thirteen

Here's a rule to always follow: Never smooch mirrors at school. You never know if the janitor uses toilet water to clean them off.

Sigmund Brouwer is the bestselling author of many books for children and young adults. Sigmund loves visiting schools and talking with youth of all ages about reading and writing. *Justine McKeen, Walk the Talk* is the second title in his new series about Justine and her efforts to create a greener community. He also has a new book for teachers and parents called *Rock & Roll Literacy*. Sigmund lives in Red Deer, Alberta, and Nashville, Tennessee.